THIS ROYAL BOOK BELONGS TO

© 2022 Sarah Smith

This is Lizzie the Queen.

Queen Lizzie has ruled England for a rather long time,
70 years to be exact.

Today is a very special day for Queen Lizzie.
It is her Platinum Jubilee!

The palace was covered with the most spectacular and sparkly decorations. The world's most delicious and delectable food had been prepared for the evening banquet. Everybody was excited about this momentous celebration.

Everybody, except Queen Lizzie.

"I know I should be excited about my Jubilee,"
said Queen Lizzie.

"But I have been Queen for 70 years. I have done everything
and I have everything,".

"I have nothing left to do!" Queen Lizzie whimpered.

The Queen had done a lot in her 70 years as a ruler.
Queen Lizzie had received

Beautiful palaces.

Queen Lizzie had
Travelled The World.

Queen Lizzie had
Met Other Kings And Queens.

Queen Lizzie had
Even Passed Laws in Parliament!

"You see, there is nothing more for me to do," sighed Queen Lizzie.

Outside the palace was a fairy, who listened to every word the Queen said.

"I know how to make this day special for the Queen," smiled the fairy.

"I will grant the Queen three wishes!"

"After all, I am a magical fairy," she said.

The fairy looked up and saw an open window and flew inside the palace.

The Queen was sitting in her office.

"Hello Queen Lizzie" said the magical fairy.

"I am your fairy princess and I am here to grant you three wishes".

Queen Lizzie paused and thought for a moment.

"Fairy, thank you for visiting me" said Queen Lizzie.

"But I can't possibly take those wishes. I have everything,".

"Are you sure, you have done everything" the
fairy eagerly replied.

"Have you jumped on your bed?
Have you stayed up all night watching movies? said the fairy.

"There must be something!" said the fairy.

"Well I have always wanted to
try go to a yoga class" said the Queen thoughtfully.

Before she knew it the Queen found herself
in a Yoga Studio.

The Queen tried different yoga poses
and stretches.

"Oh, I love this yoga class" Queen Lizzie told
the Fairy. "I feel so relaxed and calm, I wouldn't
mind having a cheeky ice-cream too,".

In a blink of an eye. Queen Lizzie
found herself outside an ice-cream
parlour, trying her favourite
ice cream flavours.

"This ice-cream is delicious!" Queen
Lizzie told the fairy.

"This day is going swimmingly well" Smiled
the Queen.

"You have one final wish" The Fairy told the
Queen. "What would you like to do?".

Queen Lizzie sat quietly and thought.

"Hmm, I know what I want," The Queen
told the Fairy.

"I want to travel to each country of
my Commonwealth, but not for duty,
for fun!"

"Your wish is granted," smiled the Fairy.

Queen Lizzie went on a safari

in South Africa.

She visited beautiful waterfalls

in Jamaica.

She even visited a rainforest in
Guyana.

After a splendid day of travelling the
world. The Queen arrived home.

"I had the most wonderful day" said Queen
Lizzie.

"I am so glad you enjoyed your day, Your
Majesty, I must go now." said The magical Fairy.

The Queen waved one last goodbye to the
Fairy and enjoyed her Platinum Jubilee celebrations.

"I guess I haven't done everything. 70 years as Queen,
here is to many more" smiled Queen Lizzie.

Printed in Great Britain
by Amazon

81103639R00022